Peppa Pig

Peppa Meets the Queen

Peppa and her family are watching television.
Suddenly there is a special announcement
from the Queen.

"The Queen! The Queen!" Peppa cheers.
"Hello to you all," the Queen says. "Today, I have
decided to give an award to the hardest-working
person in the country."

"The hardest-working person in the country is . . . Miss Rabbit!"

At the supermarket, Miss Rabbit
is closing the shop when
Mr Zebra the Postman presents
her with a golden letter.

Miss Rabbit,

Please come to my
palace to get a medal
for all your hard work.
Bring friends.

All the best,
The Queen

"I can't visit the Queen! I've got too much work to do!" Miss Rabbit panics.
"Don't worry," Peppa says. "The Queen has made it a holiday!"

Today is the day that Miss Rabbit
is going to visit the Queen.
Peppa and her friends are going, too.
"We're off to see the Queen!
We're off to see the Queen!
Eee-aye-addy-oh!
We're off to see the Queen!"
"Here we are!" Miss Rabbit squeaks.

"Look at all the fancy stuff!
Woof!" Danny Dog says.
"Don't touch anything!"
Miss Rabbit warns.

"Where is the Queen?" Emily Elephant asks.
"Quee-een!" Suzy Sheep calls. "Where are you?"

In another fancy room, there is a lady
sitting on a throne, knitting.
"Hello!" Peppa says. "Have you seen the Queen today?"
"I AM the Queen!" the lady says.

"The children are very excited to meet you, Your Majesty," says Miss Rabbit.

"I'm excited to meet all of you!" the Queen says,
standing up. "And now for Miss Rabbit's medal!
This is the Queen's Award for Industry.
Keep up the good work!"

The Queen puts a shiny gold medal
over Miss Rabbit's head.
"Cheers for Miss Rabbit!" the Queen says. "Hip hip!"
"Hooray!" shout the children.

Miss Rabbit and the children wear their boots
to go out into the palace gardens with the Queen.
"Do you play in your garden all the time,
Your Majesty?" Danny Dog asks.

"I don't have time for playing, no,"
answers the Queen.

She suddenly stops. "Oh dear! A muddy puddle.
Never mind. We can walk round it."
"You can't walk round a muddy puddle!" Peppa says.

"You have to jump in it!"
Peppa shows the Queen
how to jump up and down
in the muddy puddle.

"I say! That does look fun," the Queen says. "Here one goes then!"
"STOP!" shouts Peppa. Everyone gasps.
"If you jump in muddy puddles," Peppa says, "you must wear your boots, Your Majesty."

The Queen goes inside and comes back
with her boots on.

Everyone loves jumping up and down in muddy puddles — including the Queen!